Johnny Kaw
A Tall Tale

By Devin Scillian and Illustrated by Brad Sneed

Sleeping Bear Press™

315 East Eisenhower Parkway, Suite 200
Ann Arbor, MI 48108
www.sleepingbearpress.com

© Sleeping Bear Press

Printed and bound in the United States.

10 9 8 7 6 5 4 3 2 1

Library of Congress Cataloging-in-Publication Data

Scillian, Devin.
Johnny Kaw : a tall tale / written by Devin Scillian ; illustrated by
Brad Sneed.
p. cm.
Summary: "Based on a fictional Kansas character, a very large Johnny
Kaw clears the plains, tames a tornado, and creates the Rocky Mountains
by throwing boulders in this original tall tale"-- Provided by publisher.
ISBN 978-1-58536-791-7
[1. Stories in rhyme. 2. Family life--Kansas--Fiction. 3. Frontier and
pioneer life--Kansas--Fiction. 4. Kansas--Fiction. 5. Tall tales.]
I. Sneed, Brad, ill. II. Title.
PZ8.3.S3953Joh 2013
[E]--dc23
2012033690

For Steve and Martha Brown

—Devin

For all my young Kansas friends

—Brad

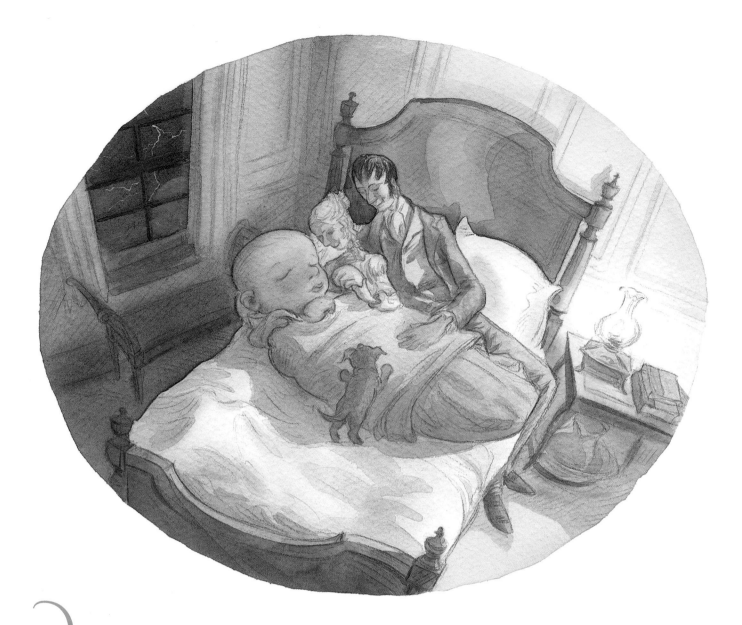

He was born on a night when a stormy wind blew;
Five minutes old, already six feet two.
And there never was a baby as big as Johnny Kaw.

That bodacious baby was the talk of the town.
Folks came to look from all around.
Seemed every hour he gained a pound.
The doctors paced and fretted and frowned.
But that baby just smiled in a crib way too small for Johnny Kaw.

Ten gallons of milk and four loaves of bread
Five or six quarts of strawberry spread
A dozen eggs, grapes by the bunch
And then a snack to hold him 'til lunch.
Ma said, "Pa, he needs room to play,
And if that boy is gonna eat this way,
We're gonna need a farm big enough for our Johnny Kaw."

So on a hot, sunny day they packed and dressed.
Pa built a wagon and pointed it west,
But there wasn't near enough room for Johnny Kaw.

The big boy laughed and said, "Pay it no mind.
I'd rather walk. I'm feeling fine."
And they left that city far behind.
Why, even the horses got to ride inside
That wagon pulled along by Johnny Kaw.

The Missouri River was plenty wide,
And by the time they reached the other side,
Papa smiled and Mama cried
For they both knew down deep inside
They had found a home for them and Johnny Kaw.

Johnny sat down to pet his big dog, Sally,
And when he got up he had made a little valley
Where Ma and Pa could build their shack.

And there on the little porch out back,
Pa hung a swing, wooden and white,
Where Ma watched the sun set every night.
And life just felt so very right to them and Johnny Kaw.

At day's first light, behind a horse and a cow,
Pa set out with a razor-sharp plow.
But each step he took seemed to rattle his bones
For the earth was full of jagged stones.
And it looked like a job for Johnny Kaw.

With his great big hands he reached down below.

He pulled up each stone, and he gave it a throw.

And in no time at all the big boy's toil

Had created the world's most perfect soil.

All those stones, as you might have guessed,

Made quite a pile way out west.

Pa just laughed when the day was done,

And the Rocky Mountains gleamed in the sun.

"All in all, it was kinda fun," laughed gentle Johnny Kaw.

Pa poked the dirt with a long-handled hoe
And thought about which crop he might grow.
Beneath a sun that was bright as brass,
Johnny was chewing on a big blade of grass.
He spat out some seeds that blew in the wind,
And before he and Pa could even begin,
There were miles and miles of wheat to tend.
"Honest to goodness, you've done it again,"
Pa said to big Johnny Kaw.

Late that day in their back-porch swing,
Pa played a fiddle and Ma would sing.
A perfect sunset fell on the plain
Over miles and miles of golden grain.
And gentle and sweet were the dreams of Johnny Kaw.

One day Pa said, "It smells like rain."
And a great wind turned the old weather vane.
Ma said, "It's fine. The wheat needs to grow."
But that mighty wind began to blow.
And blow, and blow, and blow—you know?
The western sky turned a wicked black,
The thunder rolled, and the lightning cracked.
And Johnny said, "I'll be right back."
He returned in a lick with a scythe he'd made
From a cottonwood trunk and a windmill blade.
He smiled at his folks and said, "Don't be afraid."
And off toward the storm ran Johnny Kaw.

That cyclone twister was five miles wide,
Ripping up trees to toss them aside.
It turned to the right and then it turned back,
And its path led right to Ma and Pa's shack.
But Johnny stood tall in the cyclone's roar,
Guarding the path to Ma and Pa's door.

He swung his scythe as he laughed out loud
And sliced the top off that cyclone cloud.
The winds died away and a rain so sweet
Fell gentle and soft on the glistening wheat,
And tickled the toes of the big bare feet of happy Johnny Kaw.

So life was perfect in every way,
With sunsets and songs to end each day.
But when Johnny's ma was old and gray,
One winter morning she passed away.
And for the first time since he'd been born,
Johnny didn't have the smile he'd worn.

And sad as he was, Pa was mostly
worried about Johnny Kaw.

But Johnny could hear her tender song
For the old woman's spirit was still so strong.
He said, "Pa, she's here. I know it's true."
And Pa said, "Son, I think so, too."
She was everywhere, and all around.
And she'd want to watch that sun go down.
Yes, sure as rain, she'd want her view,
So Johnny Kaw knew what to do.

He cleared every tree and left Kansas bare
So she could see that sunset from anywhere.
Up through Nebraska, across the Platte,
Tree after tree was knocked down flat.
Into the Dakotas, to the Great White North,
He swung his scythe back and forth.
Across Oklahoma and down Texas way,
And lo and behold, at the end of the day,
The golden beam of the sun's last ray
Shone on the prairie, and in the smile of Johnny Kaw.

And wherever she was, she was smiling, too.
And Pa, and Sally, and me and you.
For those fields of gold and skies of blue
Still shine each morning and glisten anew,
Because that crib and that city were way too small

for Johnny Kaw.